O9-ABI-755

MAY 1993	DATE		

09/25/03

MAY 1993

© THE BAKER & TAYLOR CO.

BABOUSHKA
AND THE THREE KINGS
by Ruth Robbins
illustrated by Nicolas Sidjakov
Adapted From A Russian Folk Tale

Parnassus Press Oakland, California
Houghton Mifflin Company   Boston

AWARDED THE CALDECOTT MEDAL AS THE MOST DISTINGUISHED AMERICAN PICTURE BOOK
FOR CHILDREN IN THE YEAR OF ITS PUBLICATION ❋❋❋❋❋❋❋❋❋❋❋❋❋❋❋

Text copyright © 1960 by Ruth Robbins   Illustrations copyright © 1960 by Nicolas Sidjakov

Library of Congress catalogue card number 60-15036   Printed in the United States of America

RNF   ISBN   0-395-27673-X
PAP   ISBN   0-395-42647-2   Y   10   9   8   7   6   5

* Long ago and far away, on a winter's evening, the wind blew hard and cold around a small hut.

✳✳✳✳✳✳✳ Inside the hut Baboushka was sweeping and scrubbing, and feeding wood to the stove. ✳ The old woman took pride in the clean comfort of her meager home.✳✳✳✳✳✳ The swirling snow drifted and deepened outside. ✳ Baboushka's hut felt snug around her; her warm stove was the center of a cold world. ✳✳ ✳✳✳✳✳✳✳✳✳✳ As day turned into night, a trumpet call sounded on the wind. ✳✳

* *

A train of travelers was approaching. Leading
the procession was a magnificent sleigh drawn
by three white horses.

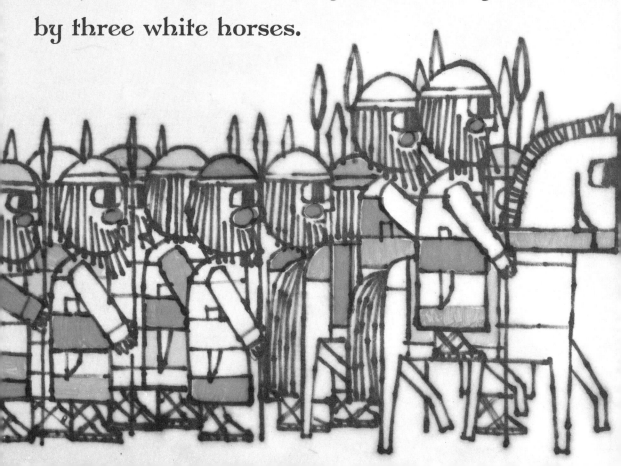

In the sleigh rode three men, splendid figures, wearing jeweled crowns and cloaks of crimson and ermine. Men on horseback followed the sleigh and behind them trudged men on foot.

✳✳✳✳ The procession stopped at the door of Baboushka's hut. Baboushka heard a knock. When she lifted the latch, the three strangers stood in the doorway. ✳✳✳ The poor woman looked in wonder at their elegant dress, their frosted beards, their kind eyes. What manner of men were these? ✳✳✳✳✳✳✳✳✳✳✳ ✳✳✳✳✳ In answer to her thought, one of the three smiled and said, "We have been following a bright star to a place where a Babe is born. Now we have lost our way in the snow. ✳✳✳

"Come with us, Baboushka. Help us to find the Child, to offer Him gifts, and to rejoice in His birth." ✳✳✳✳ ✳✳ Baboushka shivered in the cold. She hugged a shawl tightly around her thin shoulders. "Good sirs, come in and warm yourselves by the stove. I've not yet finished my day's work. ✳ And I shudder to go out on such a cruel night. Morning is wiser than evening. Rest here this night and I will go with you in the dawn."✳✳✳

✳ ✳✳✳✳ ✳✳✳✳✳✳ ✳✳✳✳✳ ✳

*** "There is no time to linger, Baboushka," answered the strangers. "If you cannot come with us now, we must continue our journey." They turned and disappeared into the storm.

✳✳✳ Baboushka went back to her sweeping and scrubbing. Her work finished, she sat down to a lonely supper close by the stove. ✳✳✳✳ The warmth of the fire reached into her heart. She felt a sudden tenderness and joy for the new born Child.✳✳✳"What grand gentlemen, those three! They did seem like kings," she said aloud. "It is no ordinary Babe they seek. Yes! I must go and follow them!" ✳✳✳✳✳✳✳ ✳✳✳ To find the new Babe, to offer Him her gift, was now her one yearning. This thought burned in her mind like a candle in the dark.

✳✳✳✳✳✳✳✳ Baboushka awoke before dawn and made ready for her journey. Into her sack she carefully placed a few poor but precious gifts. ✳✳✳ As the new day began, she stepped out onto the quiet snow. ✳✳ The old woman hunted for the path

made by the travelers, but the snow had covered their way. ✳ Stopping one person, then another, and still another, she asked, "In which direction did the three kings go; they who were seeking the Child?" ✳ Neither old nor young could tell her. ✳✳✳✳ ✳✳ Baboushka stood watching the children at play in the new snow, the dogs yelping and dancing around her. ✳✳✳ But she must not delay; she must push her way ahead. ✳ ✳

✳✳✳✳✳✳✳✳✳✳✳✳✳✳✳✳✳

✳✳✳✳✳✳ From village to village, from door to door, she went, asking, "Have you seen the Child?" Always she received the same answer; no one had seen Him. ✳✳✳✳✳✳✳✳✳ Never stopping, Baboushka wandered on searching for the Child, but never finding Him.✳✳✳✳✳✳

✳✳✳✳✳✳✳✳ And it is said that every year, at the season when the birth of the Child was first heralded, Baboushka renews her search across that land with new hope.✳✳✳✳✳✳✳✳

*********And it is said that every year little children await the coming of Baboushka. They find joy in the poor but precious gifts she leaves behind her in the silent night. *****

BABOUSHKA ✳✳ ✳✳ verse by Edith M. Thomas
✳✳ music by Mary Clement Sanks

Ba- boushka sits be- fore the fire Up- on a win- ter's night;

The driv-ing winds heap up the snow Her hut is snug and tight;

The howl-ing winds, they on- ly make Ba- boush-ka's fire more bright!

She hears a knocking at the door;
  So late — who can it be?
She hastes to lift the wooden latch,
  No thought of fear has she;
The wind-blown candle in her hand
  Shines out on strangers three.

Their beards are white with age, and snow
  That in the darkness flies;
Their floating locks are long and white
  But kindly are their eyes
That sparkle underneath their brows
  Like stars in frosty skies.

"Baboushka, we have come from far,
  We tarry but to say,
A little Prince is born this night
  Who all the world shall sway.
Come join the search, come, go with us,
  We go our gifts to pay."

Baboushka shivers at the door;
  "I would I might behold
The little Prince who shall be King
  But ah! the night is cold,
The wind so fierce, the snow so deep,
  And I, good sirs, am old."

The strangers three, no word they speak,
  But fade in snowy space!
Baboushka sits before her fire,
  And dreams, with wistful face:
"I would that I had questioned them,
  So I the way might trace!"

The morning came, and staff in hand,
  She wandered in the snow,
She asked the way of all she met,
  But none the way could show.
"It must be farther yet," she sighed:
  "Then farther will I go."

And still 'tis said, on Christmas Eve,
  When high the drifts are piled,
With staff, with basket on her arm,
  Baboushka seeks the Child:
At every door her face is seen,
  Her wistful face and mild!

Her gifts at every door she leaves:
  She bends and murmurs low,
Above each little face half-hid
  By pillows white as snow:
"And is He here?" Then, softly sighs,
  "Nay, farther must I go!"